W9-AUD-707

For Hannah,
all-by-herself
M. W.

For Georgie,
and Eddie Huntley
P. B.

Text copyright © 1992 by Martin Waddell
Illustrations copyright © 1992 by Patrick Benson

All rights reserved. No part of this book may be reproduced, transmitted, or stored in an information retrieval system in any form or by any means, graphic, electronic, or mechanical, including photocopying, taping, and recording, without prior written permission from the publisher.

U.S. 25th anniversary edition 2017

Library of Congress Cataloging-in-Publication Data is available.
Library of Congress Catalog Number 91-58750

ISBN 978-1-56402-101-4 (original hardcover edition)
ISBN 978-0-7636-9519-4 (25th anniversary edition)

APS 22 21 20 19 18 17
10 9 8 7 6 5 4 3 2 1

Printed in Humen, Dongguan, China

This book was typeset in Caslon Antique.
The pictures in this book were done with black ink and watercolor crosshatching.

Candlewick Press
99 Dover Street
Somerville, Massachusetts 02144

visit us at www.candlewick.com

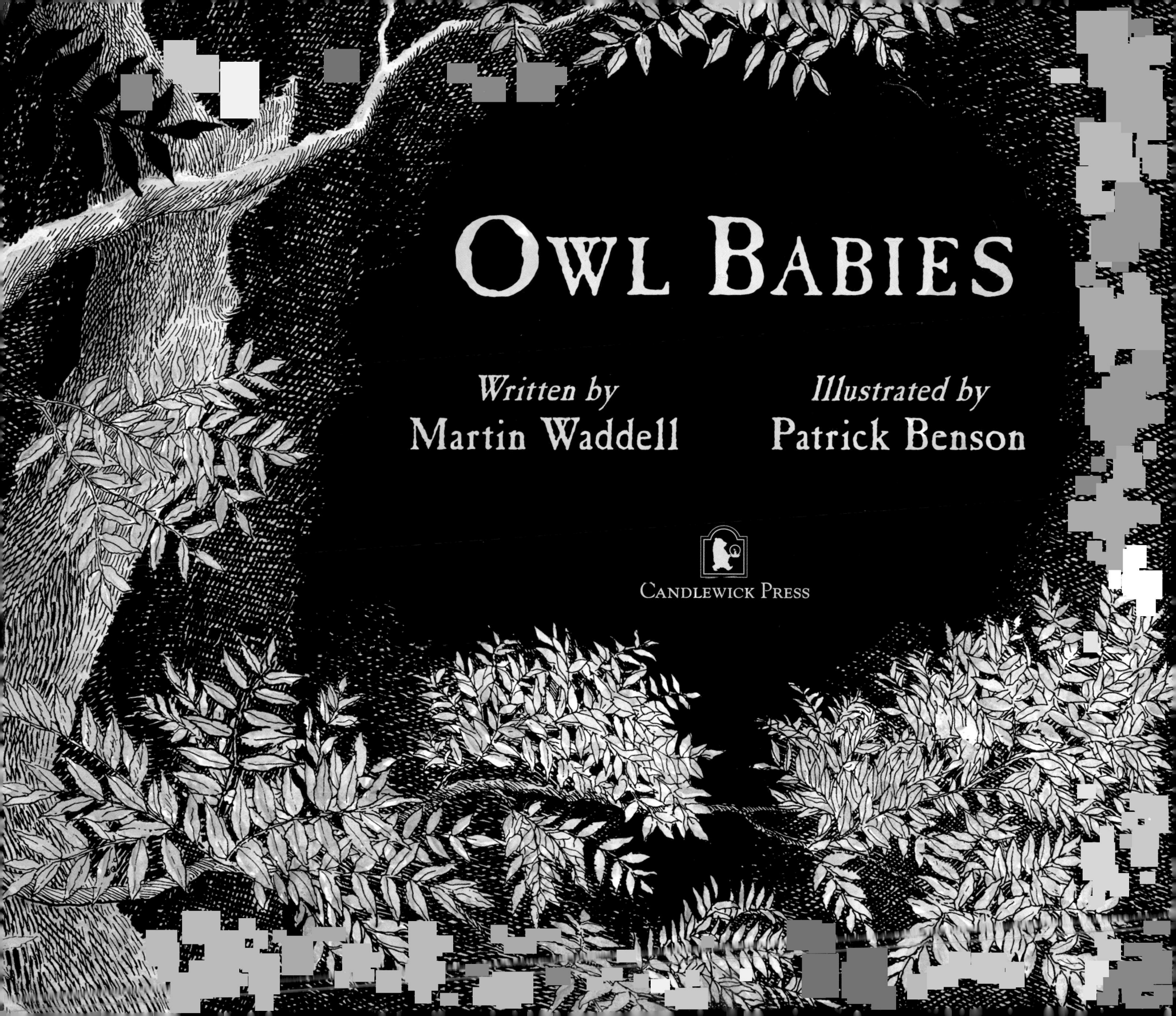

Owl Babies

Written by
Martin Waddell

Illustrated by
Patrick Benson

Candlewick Press

Once there were three baby owls:
Sarah and Percy and Bill.
They lived in a hole
in the trunk of a tree
with their Owl Mother.
The hole had twigs and
leaves and owl feathers in it.
It was their house.

One night they woke up and
their Owl Mother was GONE.
"Where's Mommy?" asked Sarah.
"Oh my goodness!" said Percy.
"I want my mommy!" said Bill.

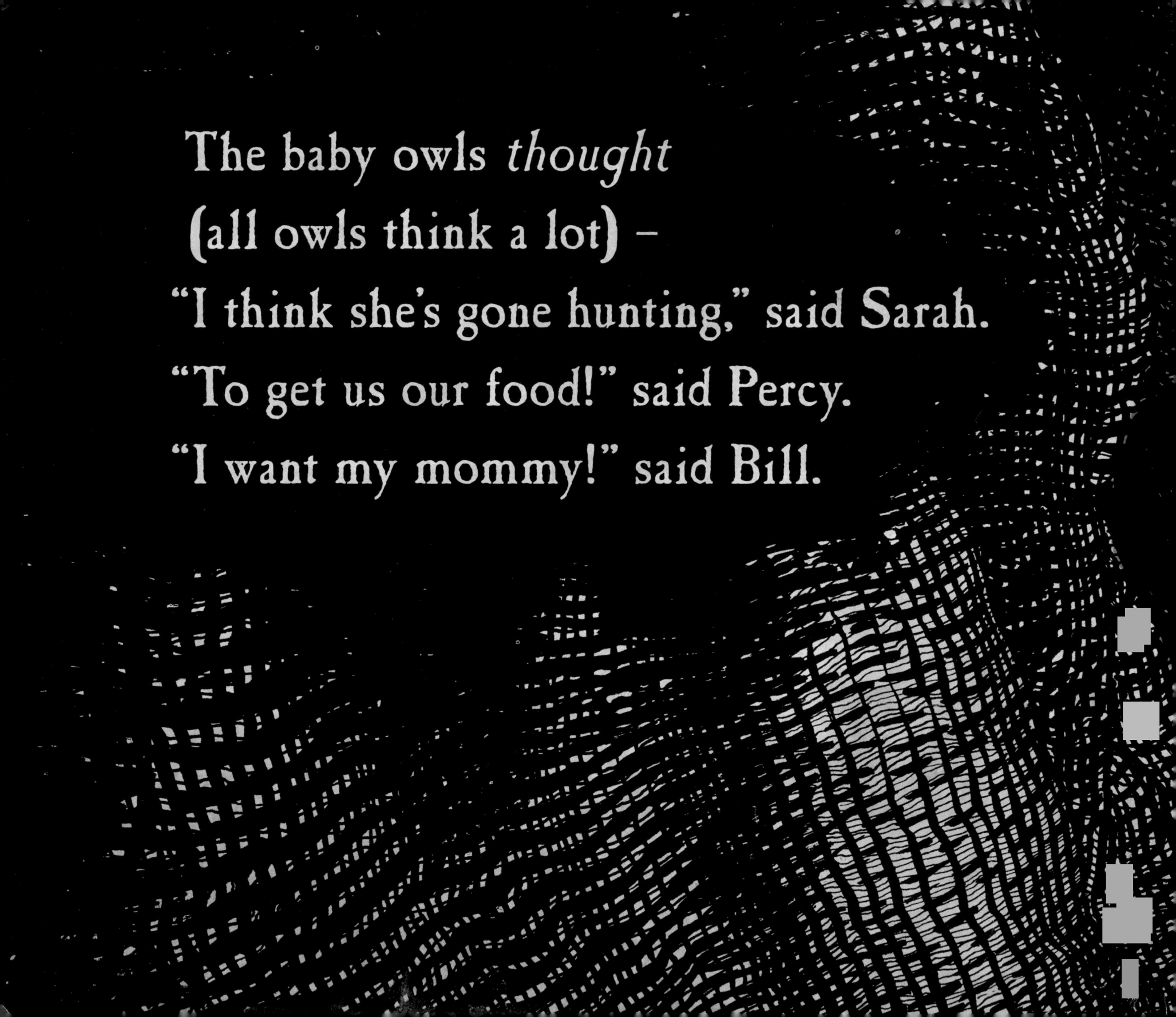

The baby owls *thought*
(all owls think a lot) –
"I think she's gone hunting," said Sarah.
"To get us our food!" said Percy.
"I want my mommy!" said Bill.

But their Owl Mother didn't come.
The baby owls came out of
their house, and they sat
on the tree and waited.

A big branch for Sarah,
a small branch for Percy,
and an old bit of ivy for Bill.
"She'll be back," said Sarah.
"Back *soon*!" said Percy.
"I want my mommy!" said Bill.

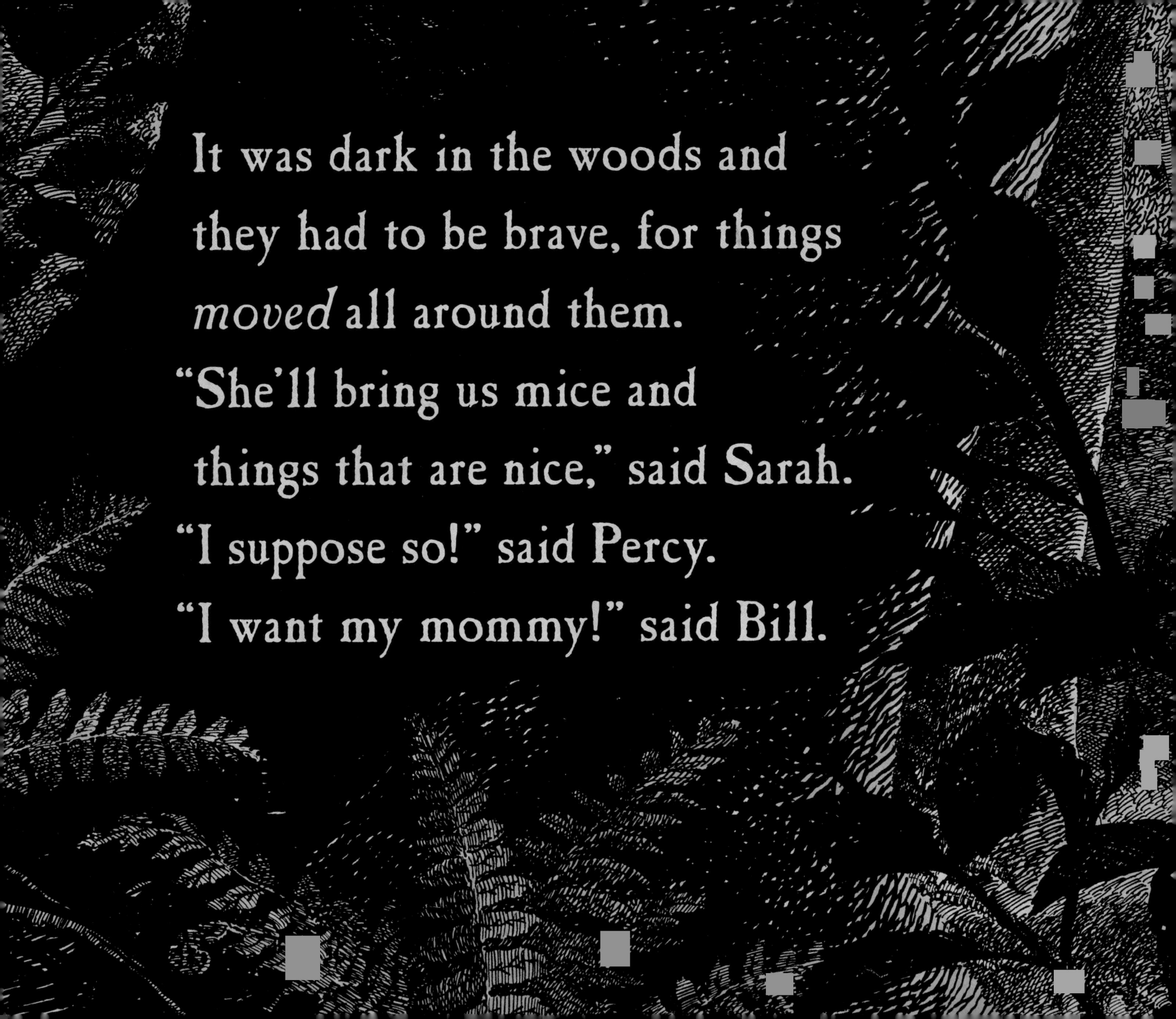

It was dark in the woods and they had to be brave, for things *moved* all around them.

"She'll bring us mice and things that are nice," said Sarah.

"I suppose so!" said Percy.

"I want my mommy!" said Bill.

They sat and they thought
(all owls think a lot) –
"I think we should *all*
sit on *my* branch," said Sarah.
And they did,
all three together.

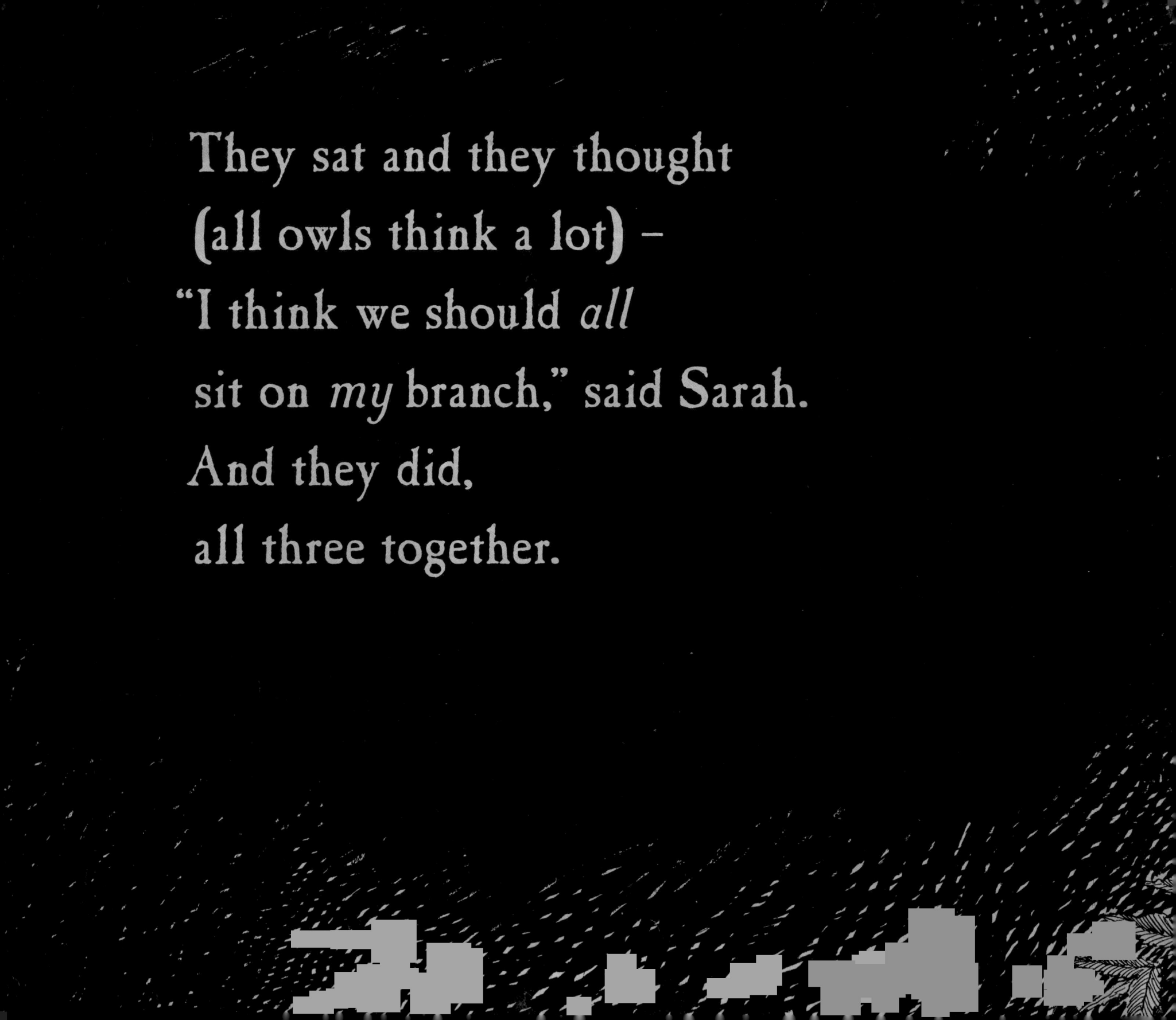

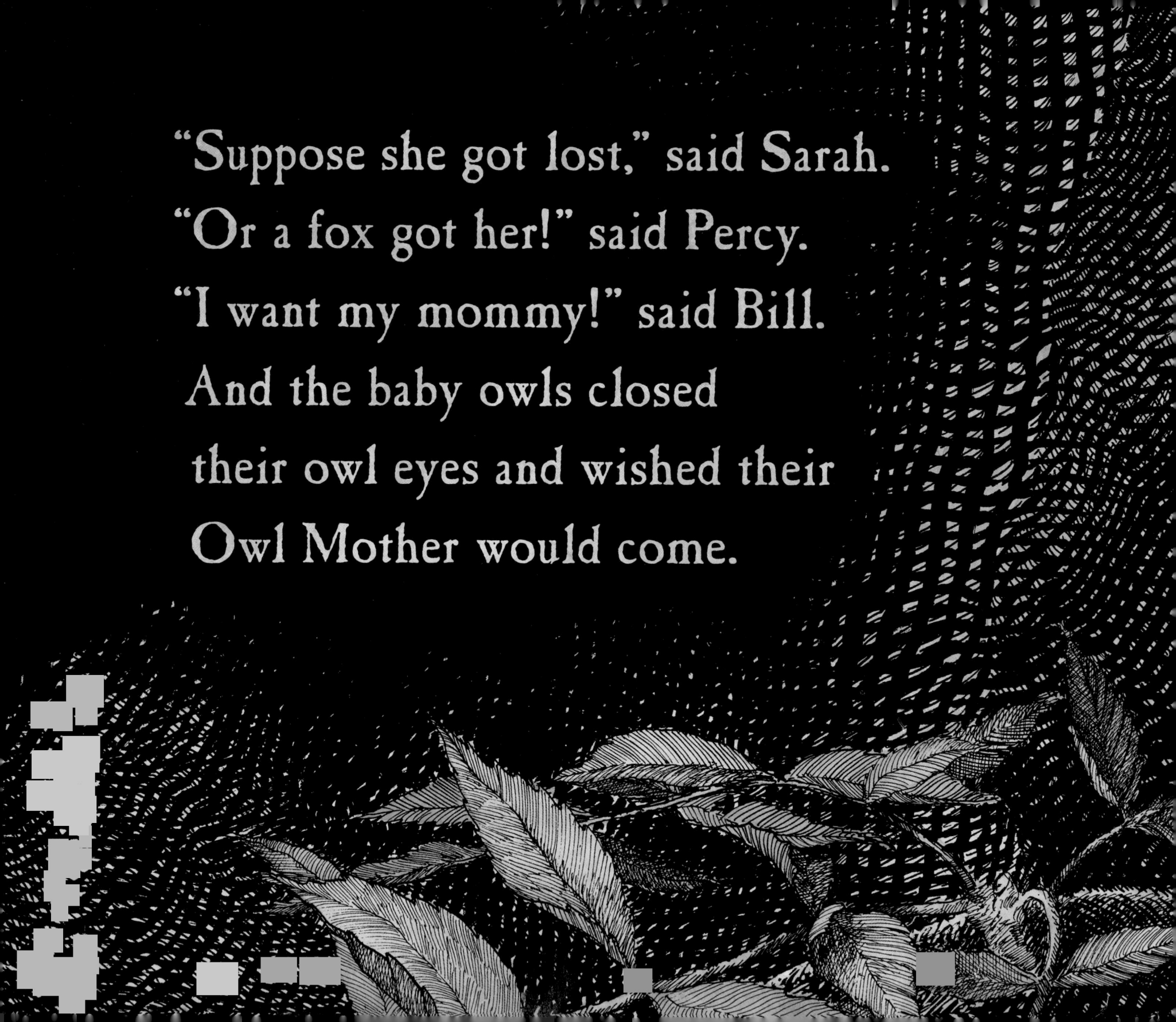

"Suppose she got lost," said Sarah.
"Or a fox got her!" said Percy.
"I want my mommy!" said Bill.
And the baby owls closed
their owl eyes and wished their
Owl Mother would come.

AND SHE CAME.

Soft and silent, she swooped
through the trees
to Sarah and Percy
and Bill.

"Mommy!" they cried,
and they flapped and they danced,
and they bounced up and down
on their branch.

"WHAT'S ALL THE FUSS?"
their Owl Mother asked.
"You knew I'd come back."
The baby owls thought
(all owls think a lot) –
"I knew it," said Sarah.
"And I knew it!" said Percy.
"I love my mommy!" said Bill.